RUPERT

MEET ALL THESE FRIENDS IN BUZZ BOOKS:

Thomas the Tank Engine
The Animals of Farthing Wood
James Bond Junior
Fireman Sam
Joshua Jones
Rupert
Babar

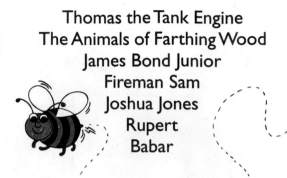

First published in Great Britain 1993 by Buzz Books,
an imprint of Reed Children's Books
Michelin House, 81 Fulham Road, London, SW3 6RB
and Auckland, Melbourne, Singapore and Toronto

ISBN 1 85591 319 4

Printed in Italy by Olivotto

RUPERT™
and the
GHOST TRAIN

Story by Norman Redfern
Illustrations by SPJ Design

One afternoon, Rupert Bear, Bill Badger
and Algy Pug went for a long walk.

"Look at Algy," laughed Bill. "A little stroll
and he's worn out!"

"I am not tired," said Algy. "I'll even race
you both home!"

Before his friends could answer, he ran
off down the lane.

"Come on, Rupert!" called Bill. "We'll
show him!"

Algy heard their footsteps coming closer
and closer. They were going to catch him!

"Whoa, there. Slow down!"

Algy skidded to a halt.

"Always in a hurry, that's the trouble with you youngsters," said Gaffer Jarge waving his walking stick angrily.

"Let's just stop for a minute," panted Algy. He was quite out of breath.

"Coming down that hill like an express train, you were," grumbled Gaffer Jarge.

"Sorry," said Rupert. "Don't you like trains, then?"

"Never been on one, and I hope I never do," replied the Gaffer. "Seen plenty, mind you. There's one on its way right now!"

"I can't hear anything," said Bill.

"Look," replied Gaffer Jarge.

In the distance, a row of little steam clouds rose above the railway line. Gaffer Jarge pulled out his old watch.

"Fast train to the South Coast," he said. "Two minutes late!"

"That reminds me," said Rupert. "Last night, I heard a train go by in the middle of the night."

"So did I," said Algy, "and the night before, too. I've never noticed it before."

"There are no trains in the middle of the night," said Gaffer Jarge. "Never have been, and I hope there never will."

"Well, I heard it!" said Bill. "Perhaps it's a ghost train!"

Rupert had an idea.

"If we all go to the station tonight, we can watch out for the mystery train," he said.

"You youngsters can go to the station tonight," said Gaffer Jarge. "I shall be tucked up snug in my bed!"

Rupert, Bill and Algy asked their parents
for permission to watch for the mysterious
train. That night they waited at Rupert's
house until it was time to go to the station.
It was very late when Mrs Bear waved
goodbye to Rupert and his friends.

"Be very careful," she told them. "And
whatever you do, make sure you don't go
near the railway line."

12

Before they had reached the garden gate,
Mrs Bear ran after them.

"Bill! Wait!" she cried. "You've forgotten
your scarf!"

Bill raced back to the cottage and put on
his warm, woollen scarf.

Rupert, Bill and Algy walked down the lane towards the station.

"We'll sit in the waiting room until we hear the train," whispered Rupert.

He walked up to the station door and turned the handle, but it was locked. Algy pressed his nose to the window.

"There's nobody there," he said, "and no more trains due until the morning!"

"Let's wait a while," said Rupert.

The three friends stood outside the station. It was very dark, and there wasn't a sound to be heard until — clunk! A strange noise came from out of the darkness.

"What was that?" asked Bill nervously.

Algy pointed towards the far end of the station platform.

"It was the signal changing," he said. "The train must be coming from Popton!"

Rupert shone his torch on the path beside the station wall.

"Look, this path runs beside the railway line all the way to Popton," he said. "Let's follow it. If we stay on this side of the fence, we'll be quite safe."

The path took Algy, Bill and Rupert through the woods. It was very dark, and the trees creaked and groaned in the breeze.

"Oh, dear," said Bill. "I hope our mystery train isn't a ghost train!"

Now the huffing and puffing of the train could be heard in the distance. Rupert leaned over the fence to look down the line. Quickly, he turned back to his friends. Something was wrong!

19

"There's a fallen tree on the line!" he cried.
"We mustn't let the train hit it!"

"What can we do?" asked Bill. "It's not
safe to go near the track!"

Rupert knew a way.

"Bill, you and Algy must run as fast as you
can to that clearing in the woods. Then..."

His friends listened carefully, then set off
along the path. As they ran away, Rupert
could hear the train rattling nearer and
nearer to the fallen tree. Then he heard a
rustling in the woods.

"What's all this fuss?" asked a cross little voice. "Why, it's Rupert!"

Suddenly, tiny doors began to open in some nearby tree trunks. The noise had woken the Imps of Spring!

"Look!" said Rupert, pointing to the railway line. "There's a tree on the line, and a train is on its way!"

"Then we must move that tree at once!" ordered a stern voice.

It was the King of the Imps.

"Algy and Bill are waiting for the train," Rupert told him. "I have a plan to stop it."

"A plan, eh?" said the King.

"Yes, and if it works, the train will stop before it reaches the tree," said Rupert.

From further down the line came a shrill whistle. Then Rupert and the King heard a screech of brakes as the heavy engine shuddered to a halt near where Bill and Algy stood.

"Forward, Imps! Forward to the fallen tree!"
cried the King, and dozens of tiny men ran
under the fence and onto the track.

"One, two, three — lift!" the King ordered.
The tree was heavy, and the Imps groaned
under its weight, but slowly it began to
move. Inch by inch they carried it to the
side of the track, where it was safely out of
the train's way. Then the little men gave a
loud cheer.

24

"What was that?" asked a strange voice.

Rupert turned round. The engine driver was marching towards him.

"My friends — " said Rupert, pointing to the far side of the track.

There was no one to be seen, although something that might have been a tiny pair of eyes glinted out of the hedgerow.

Rupert smiled to himself.

"My friends moved that tree off the line for you," he explained.

The driver was very puzzled.

"They must be very strong," he said. "It's lucky you were here to warn me about the fallen tree. And that plan of yours was very clever!"

"See how well it works!" said Bill.

26

He took off his scarf and stretched it over the end of his torch so that a red light shone brightly.

"That's a stop signal if ever I saw one!" laughed the driver.

"If you're not a ghost train," said Rupert, "then why are you out so late at night?"

"Come back to the wagons and see for yourselves," replied the driver.

27

Rupert, Bill and Algy followed the driver
down the path to the first of the trucks.

"Special service," said the driver. "It's
Mother's Day tomorrow, and the markets
need all the flowers they can get."

He opened the wagon door.

"Here you are," he said, "three bunches of
fresh flowers!"

"Thank you," replied the three friends.

"Wish your mothers each a happy Mother's Day from me!" the driver added.

Rupert, Bill and Algy had begun to walk back to Nutwood when the engine driver called them back.

"Don't forget your scarf, Bill! You never know when you might need it!"